U0022512

快快睡！豬小弟！

Go to sleep, Little Pig!

Moira Butterfield 著

Rachael O'Neill 繪

Copyright © 1990 Teeney Books Ltd.

The farmer has had a busy day on Little Farm. He has milked the cows and tidied up the hay barn. Now it's time for him to put away the tractor.

農夫在小小農場裡度過了忙碌的一天。他幫母牛擠過奶，還把穀倉裡的乾草給弄整齊了。現在該是他停放拖曳機的時候了。

The sun is sinking down behind a hill and the stars are coming out. "My goodness, I'm tired," says the farmer. "I'm looking forward to a good night's sleep!"

太陽正漸漸下山，星星也都出來了。「天哪！我真的好累好累哦！」農夫自言自語地說。「真想好好地睡一覺！」

It is time for the farm animals to go to bed, too. Look, Little Lamb is already fast asleep in the straw. He is dreaming of green fields and sunshine.

這時也是農場裡的小動物們該睡覺的時候了。你看，羊咩咩已經在稻草堆上睡得好香好熟了。他正夢見綠色的田野和溫暖的陽光呢！

But one little animal does not want to go to sleep. "I'm not tired," says Little Pig. "So I'm NOT going to bed yet. I want to stay awake and play!"

可ㄎㄜˇ是ㄕˋ呢ㄋㄜ˙，有ㄧㄡˇ一ㄧ隻ㄓ小ㄒㄧㄠˇ動ㄉㄨㄥˋ物ㄨˋ卻ㄑㄩㄝˋ不ㄅㄨˋ願ㄩㄢˋ意ㄧˋ去ㄑㄩˋ睡ㄕㄨㄟˋ覺ㄐㄧㄠˋ。「我ㄨㄛˇ不ㄅㄨˊ累ㄌㄟˋ呀ㄧㄚ˙！」豬ㄓㄨ小ㄒㄧㄠˇ弟ㄉㄧˋ說ㄕㄨㄛ。「所ㄙㄨㄛˇ以ㄧˇ我ㄨㄛˇ還ㄏㄞˊ不ㄅㄨˋ想ㄒㄧㄤˇ睡ㄕㄨㄟˋ覺ㄐㄧㄠˋ。我ㄨㄛˇ要ㄧㄠˋ保ㄅㄠˇ持ㄔˊ清ㄑㄧㄥ醒ㄒㄧㄥˇ去ㄑㄩˋ玩ㄨㄢˊ耍ㄕㄨㄚˇ！」

"Lie down, Little Pig," says Mother Pig. "There is a warm pile of clean straw for you to sleep on." "No, I won't," says Little Pig. "I want to stay awake and play!"

「躺下下，我的乖寶寶。」豬媽媽說。「這裡有一堆乾淨、溫暖的稻草可以讓你當床睡哦！」「不要！我不睡覺！」豬小弟說。「我要保持清醒去玩耍！」

"If you lie down, I'll tell you a bedtime story about the day a pig became King," says Mother Pig. "No," says Little Pig. "I'm going to stay awake and play!"

「如果你乖乖躺下睡覺的話，我就會在床邊告訴你一個故事，在某一天，有一隻小豬變成國王……」豬媽媽說。「不要啦！」豬小弟說。「我要保持清醒去玩耍！」

"All right. You can stay awake, but you'll be on your own," says Mother Pig. Then all the other animals go to sleep, one by one, except for Little Pig.

「好吧！你可以不睡覺，可是你就只能自己一個人囉！」豬媽媽說。不久之後，所有的動物一個接著一個都去睡覺了，只剩下豬小弟自己一個人。

"Wake up, Little Hen," says Little Pig. "Let's play hide and seek." But Little Hen doesn't hear him. She is asleep in the straw, dreaming of big round brown eggs.

「醒醒啊！小母雞！」豬小弟說。「我們來玩捉迷藏吧！」可是小母雞並沒有聽見豬小弟說的話。她正睡在稻草堆中，夢見一堆又大又圓的黃雞蛋呢！

"Wake up, Little Puppy," says Little Pig. "Let's play hide and seek." But Little Puppy doesn't hear him. He is asleep in his corner, dreaming of burying bones.

「起床啦！小狗狗！」豬小弟說。「我們來玩捉迷藏囉！」可是小狗狗並沒有聽見豬小弟說的話。他正睡在他的角落裡，夢見他在埋一大堆的骨頭呢！

"I'll sing a song," says Little Pig. "Baaa, baaa, black sheep... What comes next, Mum?" But Mother Pig doesn't hear him. She is asleep, dreaming about red apples.

「我要唱歌。」豬小弟說。「叭！叭！黑綿羊……媽媽，接下來該怎麼唱呢？」可是豬媽媽並沒有聽見豬小弟在說些什麼。她也已經睡著了，正夢見許多許多的紅蘋果呢！

Little Pig can see the moon's face in a puddle. "I'll catch you, moon!" he says. He jumps into the water, but the moon disappears with a splash.

豬小弟從小水窪裡看見月亮的臉蛋兒。「月亮啊！我要捉你囉！」他說。他跳進小水窪裡，可是月亮卻嘩啦的一聲不見了。

Barn Owl is sitting on her tree. "Come and play," says Little Pig. Barn Owl frowns and blinks an eye. "I'm too grown up to play silly games with you," she says.

穀倉裡的貓頭鷹正坐在樹梢上。「來玩吧！」豬小弟說。貓頭鷹皺了皺眉頭，眨了眨一隻眼睛對他說：「我已經太老了，沒法兒和你玩這些小孩子的遊戲啦！」

Oh dear. There is no-one to play with Little Pig. He looks at his own face in the puddle. "I don't care," he says to himself. "I'm going to play on my own."

哎呀！真可憐！都沒有人陪豬小弟玩吔。他看著自己映在小水窪中的臉，自言自語地說：「沒關係！我可以自己玩。」

Little Pig peeks into the cowshed and rolls on the straw. He makes funny faces at the cows. They can't see him because they have their eyes shut tight!

豬小弟往牛棚裡偷看了一下，便在稻草堆上打起滾來。他朝著母牛扮鬼臉。母牛們可看不見豬小弟在做什麼，因為她們的眼睛都緊緊地閉著哩！

Little Pig starts to yawn. "I WON'T go to bed," he says, "I'm going to count the stars. One, two, three, four..." He falls fast asleep.

豬小弟開始打起呵欠來了。「我不要睡覺。」他說。「我要數星星。一顆，二顆，三顆，四顆……」豬小弟數著數著竟然睡著了。

"Cock-a-doodle-do!" cries Cockerel the next morning. The farmer brings food for the animals, but Little Pig is still asleep. He is going to miss his breakfast!

隔天早上，「喔喔喔！」小公雞用力地大叫。農夫帶著食物來給小動物們吃。可是，豬小弟竟然還在睡覺呢！他快要吃不到早餐囉！

"Wake up, Little Pig," says Little Lamb. "Let's go to the field and hunt for daisies!" But Little Pig is too tired to play. He went to bed too late last night.

「醒醒啊！豬小弟。」羊咩咩叫他。「我們到草地上去找小雛菊吧！」可是啊，豬小弟實在是太疲倦，沒有力氣去玩了。因為他昨天晚上太晚睡覺啦！

Oh dear, Little Pig is tired all day. He feels awful and he is in a terrible bad temper. When his friends come to see him he is very rude. "Go away!" he shouts.

哎呀！情況不妙囉！豬小弟整天都覺得好累。他感覺很不好而且脾氣也變得很暴躁。當他的朋友們來看他的時候，他表現得很沒有禮貌。他大吼著叫他們「走開！」

"Are you going to stay awake tonight?" says Mother Pig. Little Pig doesn't hear her. He has gone to bed early, and he is so tired that he doesn't even dream!

「你今天晚上還是不睡覺嗎？」豬媽媽說。可是豬小弟根本沒聽見媽媽說的話，因為他早就已經睡著了。豬小弟實在是太累了，累得連個夢都沒有呢！